Put Beginning Readers on the Right Track with ALL ABOARD READING™

The All Aboard Reading series is especially for beginning readers. Written by noted authors and illustrated in full color, these are books that children really and truly *want* to read—books to excite their imagination, tickle their funny bone, expand their interests, and support their feelings. With four different reading levels, All Aboard Reading lets you choose which books are most appropriate for your children and their growing abilities.

Picture Readers—for Ages 3 to 6
Picture Readers have super-simple texts, with many nouns appearing as rebus pictures. At the end of each book are 24 flash cards—on one side is the rebus picture; on the other side is the written-out word.

Level 1—for Preschool through First-Grade Children
Level 1 books have very few lines per page, very large type, easy words, lots of repetition, and pictures with visual "cues" to help children figure out the words on the page.

Level 2—for First-Grade to Third-Grade Children
Level 2 books are printed in slightly smaller type than Level 1 books. The stories are more complex, but there is still lots of repetition in the text, and many pictures. The sentences are quite simple and are broken up into short lines to make reading easier.

Level 3—for Second-Grade through Third-Grade Children
Level 3 books have considerably longer texts, harder words, and more complicated sentences.

All Aboard for happy reading!

For Laura Driscoll,
who spells everything right—J.H.

Library of Congress Cataloging-in-Publication Data

Abby Cadabra, super speller / by Joan Holub.
    p. cm. — (All aboard reading. Level 2)
    Summary: Abby is the best speller in the class until a new witch shows up at school and the two of them compete in a spelling bee to see who will win a new broomstick.
    [1. Witches—Fiction. 2. English language—Spelling—Fiction.] I. Title. II. Series.
    PZ7.H7427 Ab 2000
    [E]—dc21
                                                                                    00-026422

ISBN 0-448-42281-6 (GB)   A B C D E F G H I J
ISBN 0-448-42168-2 (pbk.)   A B C D E F G H I J

ALL
ABOARD
READING™

Level 2
Grades 1-3

Abby Cadabra, Super Speller

By Joan Holub

Grosset & Dunlap • New York

Abby Cadabra was a super speller.

She could spell short words

like C-A-T and T-O-A-D.

And she could spell longer words

like S-P-I-D-E-R, too.

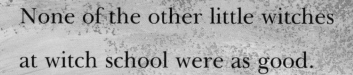

None of the other little witches

at witch school were as good.

Then one day, at thirteen o'clock,
a new little witch showed up.

Ms. Poof clapped her hands.

"Class," she said,

"this is Wanda Cassandra."

Wanda sat down

next to Abby.

Abby saw a pin on Wanda's hat.

"That's my spelling medal,"

Wanda bragged.

"I was the best speller at
my old school."

Abby rolled her eyes.

Wanda was going to be

<u>second</u> best around here.

"That reminds me," said Ms. Poof.

"We are having a spelling bee tomorrow!"

The little witches gulped.

Spelling bees at witch school

were extra hard.

First each little witch

had to spell a word.

Then she had to say

why it was spelled that way.

And <u>then</u> she had to use the word

in a magic spell!

Ms. Poof said,

"The best speller will win

a very special prize."

She got something out of the closet.

"It is a rocket-powered flying broom!"

Abby gazed at the broom

with love in her eyes.

But Wanda said,

"Don't count your brooms

before they zoom.

Because I am going to win.

Just wait and see."

Abby did not want to wait and see.

She had to find out how good

Wanda's spelling was <u>now</u>.

So after school,

she followed Wanda home.

She peeked in Wanda's window.

Wanda was working on her spelling.

"W-I-N-N-I-N-G," Wanda spelled.

Then she said the rule:

"If the last letter is a consonant,

double it so there are two

before you add a suffix

that starts with A, E, I, O, or U.

Win—double N,

add I-N-G—

make me the winning witch

of the school spelling bee."

Zzzzap! A big bee appeared.

It sprinkled magic dust

all over Wanda.

The magic dust would make her win.

That was cheating!

Abby jumped through the window.

"No fair!" she yelled at Wanda.

Wanda spun around.

"Snoop!" she shouted at Abby.

"C-H-E-A-T-E-R,"

Abby spell-yelled.

"Sometimes two letters

make just one sound,

like in words where

the letters CH are found.

Cheater, cheater,

I declare!

I see Wanda's underwear!"

A breeze blew around Wanda.

It blew until her long undies showed.

"I bet you can't win

fair and square!" Abby said.

Wanda frowned.

"Can, too!" she said.

"I'll undo my winning spell.

And we'll just see who wins!"

So Wanda called off her spell.

And Abby zipped home

to work on her spelling.

At school the next day,

the spelling bee began first thing.

An hour later, only two witches

were still standing—

Abby and Wanda.

Both of them had spelled

every word correctly so far.

Ms. Poof called on Abby.

"Spell FROGS," she said.

Abby spelled, "F-R-O-G-S."

She said the rule:

"Add S to most words

to show two or more.

One frog, two frogs,

three frogs, four!"

Then she cast her magic spell.

Hippity! Ploppity! Hop!

Four frogs appeared.

They leaped all over Wanda.

Wanda screamed.

Abby smiled.

Her spell had worked!

Ms. Poof turned to Wanda.

"Spell FRIEND," she told her.

Wanda spelled,

"F-R-I-E-N-D.

I before E

except after C,

or when pronounced 'ay'

as in NEIGHBOR and WEIGH."

Now came her magic spell.

"Little furry black bat,

do you want to be my friend?

Then fly around that witch's hat

and land upon its end."

Itchy! Twitchy!

A cute little bat flew into the room.

It sat on the tip of Abby's hat.

Everyone clapped.

Abby felt silly.

Back and forth

and back and forth.

Abby and Wanda spelled

all morning.

29

Then Ms. Poof said to Abby,

"Spell BROOMSTICK."

Gadzooks! thought Abby.

A compound word!

Abby wiggled her ears

and thought hard.

Then she took a deep breath.

"B-R-O-O-M-S-T-I-K,"

she spelled.

Ms. Poof stopped Abby.

"I'm sorry," she said kindly.

"But that is not correct.

Wanda, can you spell it?"

Oh no! thought Abby.

Now Wanda was going to win!

Wanda twitched her nose

and thought hard.

"B-R-U-M-S-T-I-C-K,"

she spelled.

Ms. Poof stopped Wanda, too.

"That is not right either,"

Ms. Poof said.

"So who won?" asked the little witches.

"We'll see," said Ms. Poof.

"Let's go to the next word...."

Just then,

Abby thought of something.

"Wait!" she cried.

She turned to Wanda.

"Come on," Abby whispered.

"I've got an idea."

Abby and Wanda

hopped on their brooms

and flew out of the classroom.

The other little witches

ran to the window to watch.

In the air,

Abby yelled over to Wanda.

"I know how to spell BROOM,"

she said.

Wanda yelled back,

"And I know how to spell STICK!"

Abby nodded.

"Let's put them together,"

said Abby.

In big sky writing,

Abby spelled:

Wanda spelled:

Then they pushed their words

closer together.

Ta-dah!

Now they spelled one big word:

BROOMSTICK.

Abby and Wanda landed their brooms

in front of the classroom window.

Together, they shouted:

"B-R-O-O-M-S-T-I-C-K!

Take two little words,

and stick them together with glue.

You'll get a compound word

that's completely new."

Then they shouted,

"Brooms for sweeping.

Broomsticks to fly.

Broomsticks! Broomsticks!

Rain from the sky!"

Bobble! Wobble! Boom!

There was thunder.

There was lightning.

And then, brand-new broomsticks

rained from the sky!

Ms. Poof smiled.

"Abby and Wanda, you both win.

You will share the prize.

You both earned it

with your super spelling

and your teamwork!"

And that was that.

Wanda flew the prize broomstick

on Mondays and Tuesdays.

She flew in zigzag lines

all around outer space.

Abby flew the broomstick
on Wednesdays and Thursdays.
She made loop-the-loops
around the moon.

And on Fridays,

Abby and Wanda shared.

Heckle, speckle,

piffity, poof.

This story's done,

and here's the proof—